Dead Flowers

Poems, Limericks and Illustrations

By Christian DeWild

ISBN-13: 978-1-7337707-3-6

For my parents

Brigitte De Wild
Andy De Wild

Edited by Stephanie Tebbs, J Palm
And Andy De Wild

Chapter I

Sweet Dreams And Guillotines

Mary's In The Mausoleum
Allister Rose From The Dead
There Was An Old Vampire
Seven Bats
Tabitha's Toes
Sad Girl
Alone
Long Stemmed And Black
The Patient Thumb Tack
Pee On My Shoes
Backwards Underwear
Toilet Paper Sheets
Dirty Blankets
Toilet Paper Spider
Nocturnal Ned
Billy Likes Worms
Mason Jars
Creepy Chris
Steering Wheel Dave
Unibrow Lester
Ophelia

Sometimes We Laugh
I Miss You
Old Pictures
Happiness Comes
I Am Free To Be
I'm Giving Up
Sometimes I'm Scared Of The Dark
Scary Portraits
Nobody But Me
The Hostile Doorbell
One Spell
Pink
Portable Wall
Some Doors
Head In The Clouds
Kaleidoscope Eyes
Resurrected Backyard Doll
Spider Bites
Halloween Is Coming
Monsters Creeping In A Row
The Haunted Ballroom
Spooky Me And Spooky You
Benjamin Bat
The Wicked Old Witch
Edgar The Vampire
Spooky Family
Mr. Grimly's Gruesome Ghost
Scary People Stories
Vicky And Vincent
Sweet Dreams And Guillotines

Chapter II

<u>Dead Flowers</u>

A Pumpkin On My Mailbox
I Had A Cat
The Little Frightened Ghost
The Haunted Ballroom
Gruesome Lester
Allister Picked A Scab
Creepy Moon
Adrift On My Sea
Drown
Another Time
Fragmented People
Black's My Favorite Color
Macabre Mary
The Morning After
Dead Flowers
Ghosts And Goblins
Crypts And Coffins
Casting Spells
Box Of Curses
Boogers And Blood
Myrmecophobia
Ear-Pierced Holes
Corn On The Cob

Chapter III

<u>Ashes To Ashes</u>

13 Ghosts
Some Ghosts
Grandpa Vampire
Grandpa's Ear
Peter Jebb
Popcorn Dish
Lost My Head Again
Perry, Perry Pumpkin Head
Putting Things Together
Close To The Bottom
We All Have Scars
Alison Sodden
Rainy Day Poem
Warming Bones
Watching Clouds
Bugs
Blood Or Ketchup
Bobby Grew Tired
Edmond Had A Hammer
Antique Vase
Mortuary Bob
Reckless Witch
Captain Dread

Chapter IV

Let's Get Married On Halloween

Let's Get Married On Halloween
Sleeping In The Graveyard
Ghost In A Jar
Mason Licked His Finger
Odds And Ends
Hair In My Ears
Let's Start Over
Happily Never After
80 Years
Happy Me
The Crow And The Rainbow
Cemetery Statue
Sixteen Little Pumpkins
Three Little Zombies
Zombie, Zombie
Bones
Broken Days
This Is For Someone
What Do You Do?
Who You Are
I Love You So Much

Bubbles In The Bath
Leland Dug Himself A Hole
Garbage Can Lollypop
Last Christmas I Got…
Bubble Gum Shoe
Rub A Dub Dub
Buzz Away Fly
Tip Toe Mosquito
Mosquitos In The Lantern Light
You Wrecked Me
Orange Peel Gentleman
Little Pink Clouds
Hello Up There Midnight Moon
As Far As My Arms Can Go
Rubber Bat
Milford The Cozy Ghost
Dangling Little Feet
Levitating Molly
The Old Tangled Tree
Victoria Drabs
Windowsill Cobwebs
Mummy With A Runny Nose
Batsicle, Ratsicle
Ghost Bat
Ghost In A Box
Plan My Funeral

Chapter I
Sweet Dreams And Guillotines

Mary's In The Mausoleum

Mary's in the mausoleum
Talking to the dead
Making sure that all of them
Are tucked into their bed

Telling scary stories
Kissing them good night
Picking up the candle stick
And blowing out the light

Allister Rose From The Dead

Allister rose from the dead
He was tired of lying in bed
He tried to lay down and sleep off his frown
But he lay there resentful instead

Fully awake in his crypt
His eyes staring up at the lid
How could this be? He now had to pee
A feeling he surely must rid

Aggrieved to be buried alive
By his friends and his family alike
They all just stood by and tossed him inside
With a tear and a mournful "good-bye"

But all of his anger toward this
For the moment he should just dismiss
His bladder was plump and ready to dump
And about to fill the abyss

He pushed wide open the lid
Dirt filled the box where he hid
He crawled from the hole that buried his soul
And ran fast as he never did

He found a place he could pee
Behind the trunk of a tree
Alone in the night and well out of sight
He was sure that no one would see

He paid the greatest expense
When he peed on the electrical fence
Shocked to his death, took his last breath
His funeral can now recommence

There Was An Old Vampire

There was an old vampire
As old as can be
So old in fact
He didn't have teeth

He hadn't a molar
He hadn't a fang
He hadn't a canine
Oh my what a shame

He was an old vampire
As old as they come
With a mouth full of nothing
Except for his gums

He couldn't suck blood
And I fear the worst
This unlucky vampire
Will soon die of thirst

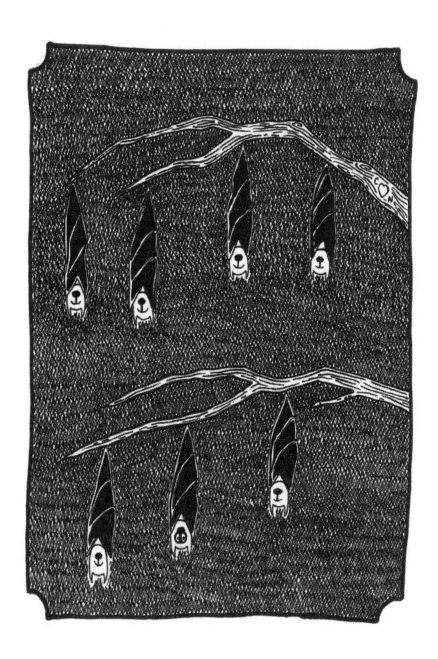

Seven Bats

Seven bats up in a tree
Six are sleeping peacefully
One's awake in agony
Had himself a scary dream

Tabitha's Toes

Tabitha's toes
Were attached to her feet
And somehow they always
Got grabbed in her sleep

She dared not to leave
Her bed late at night
Of fear upon losing
Her toes to a bite

Sad Girl

Sad girl
With her rainy eyes
Never liked
Long goodbyes

People came
But then they'd leave
Sad girl stayed
And sad girl grieved

<u>Alone</u>

I enjoy being alone
I don't enjoy being lonely

Long Stemmed And Black

Some roses are red
But I take those back
And exchange them for roses
Long stemmed and black

The Patient Thumb Tack

The patient thumb tack
Waited alone
Lost in the carpet
Inside of my home
Yes, lost in the carpet
Finely concealed
From my fully exposed
Barefooted heal

Pee On My Shoes

Pee on my shoes
Pee on my shoes
What do I do
With pee on my shoes

It wasn't intended
It's not what I do
But somehow I got
Pee on my shoes

Backwards Underwear

My underwear's on backwards
My socks are inside out
My shirt is on the wrong way
And my pants cannot be found

The bus is on its way
To take me to my school
I'll either start a brand new trend
Or just be ridiculed

Toilet Paper Sheets

I feel sorry for the cotton plants
That grow up to be toilet paper sheets
It's an unfortunate task at hand
A very unfortunate task indeed

These soft little cotton toilet sheets
Have a most troublesome job to do
The lucky sheets take care of one
The unlucky ones, number two

Dirty Blanket

Dirty blanket
You stink
You make my eyes
Water and blink
My nose, it bunches
My stomach, it hunches
I'm ready to
Puke in the sink

Dirty blanket
You need to be washed
Tumbled in water
And tossed
Hung up and then dried
Till everything died
And all of your
Stink has been lost

Dirty blanket
You're gross
You make me
Curl my toes
You're tattered and torn
Completely out worn
You need to be
Tossed out and hosed

Toilet Paper Spider

Toilet paper spider
I thought that you were dead
I pinched you between two pieces of ply
But you fell out and ran off instead

<u>Nocturnal Ned</u>

Nocturnal Ned
Feasts on dead
Little insects
By his bed

Chews them up
In little bits
That he mixes
Up with spit

Serves it up
In bottle caps
To his little
Friendly rats

Nocturnal Ned
Feasts on dead
Little insects
By his bed

Billy Likes Worms

Billy likes worms
He likes the way they play
He likes the way they look
When they move about the day

He likes the way they feel
And he likes their lack of haste
But what Billy likes the most
Is the way that they all taste

Mason's Jars

Mason liked jars
All different kinds
He'd fill them up
With things he'd find

One had a foot
He found in a lake
The foot was attached
To a passionate snake

One had a tie
Of impeccable thread
But upon further scrutiny
It came with a head

One of these jars
Appeared to be bare
With only a label
"Please handle with care"

Here is a jar
Labeled "From Bart"
It seems to be housing
A 3 year old fart

Creepy Chris

Creepy Chris
Was in bliss
Staring at a bowl of fish

They were dead
And underfed
Floating upside down instead

Still he stared
Never dared
Turning his gaze anywhere

Creepy Chris
Was in bliss
Staring at his floating fish

Steering Wheel Dave

Steering Wheel Dave
Walked near and walked far
With a steering wheel
But never a car

He walked and he steered
With his hands on the wheel
Turned as he signaled
And always would yield

He drove himself walking
With hands ten and two
Until his flat tire
I mean, worn out shoe

Unibrow Lester

Unibrow Lester
Thought it unfair
That both of his eyes
Were expected to share

Share his one eyebrow
His forehead mustache
His frontal coiffure
His cranium sash

<u>Ophelia</u>

Ophelia had her heart tossed about
She decided to make a game
So she hurt all the people she thought she loved
So they couldn't do the same

Sometimes We Laugh

Sometimes we laugh
Sometimes we cry
Sometimes we throw up
Our arms and just sigh

Sometimes we do
Sometimes we don't
Sometimes we're just
Unwilling and won't

Sometimes we whisper
Sometimes we yell
Sometimes we lift up
Others who fell

Sometimes we take
Sometimes we give
Sometimes we give all
So others may live

I Miss You

I miss you when you're gone
I miss you when you're here
I miss you when you're far
I miss you when you're near
I miss you all the time
I don't know why I do
I miss you when I'm not
Standing next to you

Old Pictures

I don't like old pictures
They remind me of things
I will never have or see again
They remind me of people
I will never meet again
Even though I still know you
You are not the same person I knew
In old pictures

Happiness Comes

No sense trying
To fit in
It's a battle
You can't win
Just be happy
In your skin
Happiness comes
From within

I Am Free To Be

I am free to be
Or not to be
Anything I wish to be
Not up to you
But up to me
Who to be or not to be
I am me
I'm not you
And you're not me
We are us
But separately
That's the way it's meant to be

I'm Giving Up

I may be down, I may be stuck
But that doesn't mean I'm giving up
There may be times I'm in a rut
But that doesn't mean I'm giving up
Sometimes I jumped instead of ducked
But that doesn't mean I'm giving up
At times I've gotten stuck in the muck
But that doesn't mean I'm giving up
My life has been a lot of bad luck
But that doesn't mean I will give up

Sometimes I'm Scared In The Dark

Sometimes I'm scared in the dark
Sometimes I'm scared in the light
Sometimes I'm scared just to be scared
And I don't know the reason why

Scary Portraits

There's a house with
Scary portraits on the walls
Scary portraits up and down the halls
Scary portraits with eyes that stare
Eyes that follow, eyes that glare

Nobody But Me

Someone writes messages
On my bathroom mirror
Steam from the shower
Make the messages appear
What I find disturbing
Haunting and weird
Is that there is nobody
But me living here

The Hostile Doorbell

The hostile doorbell
When pressed would say
"What do you want?
Just go away!
Leave us be,
And don't return!
Hit the road.
Be adjourned.
Don't tread lightly.
Run away.
Do anything,
But just don't stay!"

One Spell

There once was a boy
Who learned a spell
Just one spell
Did he learn very well

He learned how to make
People sneeze
Whenever he wanted
Whenever he pleased

To him it was fun
To him it was play
He found it quite joyful
To cause disarray

He caused children to sneeze
Macaroni and cheese
Out of their nose
With the greatest of ease

Pink

Pink is for candy
That's so nice and dandy
Pink is for gum
And hours of fun
Pink is for lipstick
You wear on your lips
Pink is for polish
And fingernail tips
Pink is for kites
High in the skies
But pink isn't good
When oozing from eyes

Portable Wall

I will invent
A portable wall
So no one can see me
No one at all

And I cannot hear
When somebody calls
And they will not hear
What I say at all

And I will be happy
With nobody here
And you will not know
That I've disappeared

You will not have
A thought or a clue
And you won't see me
And I won't see you

I'll travel around
With my portable wall
I'll visit New Prague
Or maybe St. Paul

And you, with no clue
Of my travels at all
For you cannot see me
Behind this here wall

Then I will come back
Feeling quite blue
Since you can't see me
And I can't see you

And we haven't seen
Each other at all
Ever since I
Put up this wall

Some Doors

Some doors are open
Some doors are closed
Some doors stand tall
In a menacing pose

Some doors are metal
Some doors are wood
Some would stay open
If they only could

Some doors are squeaky
And I think you'd agree
That some doors get slammed
When kids get angry

Some doors are crooked
And never close right
Sometimes I hear mine
Squeak open at night

Some doors have latches
Others have locks
Prehistoric people
Closed caves with big rocks

Some doors have a peephole
For a small glimpse outside
My neighbors don't like me
So they peek and then hide

Some doors are rectangle
Some are just square
Some may be circles
But those are quite rare

Some doors are mental
And hard to construe
They take most of a life time
Before you get through

Head In The Clouds

Head in the clouds
Head in the clouds
Why do I always
Have my head in the clouds?

Even though I
Have my feet on the ground
I still manage to keep
My head in the clouds

Kaleidoscope Eyes

One night
Gazing out my window
Up at the trees
Underneath the moon glow

I spotted two eyes
Staring at me from the trees
I spied them
And they spied me

I shifted my gaze
Then spotted four
Then there were six,
Eight and two more

Ten tree top eyes
Staring at me
Alone in my bed
Too frightened to sleep

Ten peering eyes
Into my room
With no good intention
Of leaving me soon

Ten glaring beasts
Perched way up high
Looking below
With kaleidoscope eyes

Throwing my covers
And pulling the shades
Keeping the light on
Till night turns to day

When those creatures above
Fly out of their trees
Then maybe I
Will then get some sleep

Resurrected Backyard Doll

Resurrected backyard doll
Your hair is quite a mess
I found you in a shallow hole
Where you were laid to rest

I should have let you stay
But I took you home instead
And ever since that very day
My life's been full of dread

You've cast a shadow on this house
And everyone inside
You never take your rest at night
And never close your eyes

Your painted smile is sinister
Your antique dress is torn
You stick into my consciousness
Just like a buried thorn

My dreams have turned to nightmares
And no one can go to sleep
Especially when we faintly hear
The patter of little feet

I curse the very day we met
And I don't know what to do
I feel that someone's watching me
In every empty room

Resurrected back yard doll
It's time I put you back
In the yard from whence you came
Before you do attack

Now I'll have to set you down
And dig and empty hole
Six or seven or eight feet deep
Toward the southern pole

My, it's gotten dark in here
This hole is now quite deep
I think it's time to climb back up
Although the walls are steep

I should have brought you down
And not dug here alone
Now it's raining dirt on me
Or is it being thrown?

"Resurrected back yard doll
You can't burry me
I'm the one that rescued you"
Quite regretfully

Resurrected backyard doll
My hair is quite a mess
You put me in a shallow hole
And now I cannot rest

Spider Bites

I don't like
Spider bites
Don't wanna quench
Their appetites
Don't wanna be
Their meal at night
I don't like
Spider bites

Halloween Is Coming

Halloween is coming
Halloween is near
Halloween is simply
My favorite time of year

Monsters Creeping In A Row

Monsters creeping in a row
Monsters creeping toe to toe
Arms unfurled and eyes a blaze
Creeping crawling through the haze

Monsters creeping in the dark
In the streets and in the park
Apparitions in the night
Through the little bits of light

Monsters creeping in a line
Only where the moonlight shines
Making shadows on the wall
Making shadows growing tall

Monsters stomping on the ground
Lock your doors they're in your town
Monsters creeping where they can
Eating from your garbage can

Monsters feasting on some rats
Monsters eating all your cats
Monsters half alive or dead
Monsters underneath your bed

Go to sleep and don't make noise
Even though they have your toys
Monsters really do not care
And most certainly don't share

Spooky Me And Spooky You

Spooky me
And spooky you
Let's go spend
The afternoon
Scaring people
From their shoes
We are ghosts
That's what we do
Spooky me
And spooky you

Benjamin Bat

Benjamin Bat
Was exactly that
A boy and a bat
As a matter of fact

He had a head
Two arms and two legs
He also had wings
Just to fly away

The Wicked Old Witch

The wicked old witch
To her cauldron did say
"Oh creepy cauldron
Tell me with haste
Who is the wickedest
Witch in this place?"

The cauldron spoke back
And said "You are my dear.
You are the wickedest
Witch around here"

The wicked old witch
To her cauldron then said
"Oh creepy cauldron"
Her eyes blazing red
"Who has the wickedest
Thoughts in her head"

The cauldron did answer
And answered quite plain
"You do my dear,
Have the wickedest brain."

The wicked old witch
To her cauldron then groaned
"Oh creepy cauldron
Then would you know
Why am I always
Completely alone?"

The cauldron said nothing
It was already known
And there cried the witch
Even now more alone

Edgar The Vampire

Edgar the vampire
Was scared of the dark
So he stayed home at night
And eventually starved

Spooky Family

Spooky me
Spooky mother
Spooky dad
Spooky brother

Spooky us
Yes indeed
Just one spooky
Family

Spooky house
Creepy trees
Lots of branches
But no leaves

Spooky mom
Goes to work
At the morgue
As a clerk

Spooky dad
Sleeps all day
But at night
He's wide awake

Being spooky
All around
In and out of
This old town

Scaring people
Just for fun
Laughing as they
Turn and run

Spooky brother
In his crib
Slobber, soaking
Up his bib

Spooky us
Yes indeed
Just one spooky
Family

Mr. Grimly's Gruesome Ghost

Mr. Grimly's
Gruesome ghost
Is the one
I see the most
I'm not scared
Of him at all
Even though
He's in the hall
I used to be
Not anymore
Even though
He's at my door
I used to be
But I am not
Even though
He's picked the lock
Opened the door
And peeked his head
Now he's sitting
On my bed

But I'm not scared
Not scared of he
Since he's my gramps
And has no teeth

Scary People Stories

Do ghosts ever have sleepovers
Where they stay up all night
Telling scary people stories
Until the morning light?

Vicky And Vincent

Vicky and Vincent
Were madly in love
They went well together
Like hands in a glove

They weren't like the rest
And not quite like most
But they sure went together
Like a spirit and ghost

They were never apart
Like doom is to gloom
As if one was a coffin
And the other a tomb

They fit well together
Like ashes and dust
Gruesome and foul
Evening and dusk

Vicky and Vincent
Were madly in love
They went well together
Like hands in a glove

Sweet Dreams And Guillotines

Sweet dreams and guillotines
Folding ends, sewing seams
This is how we all come clean
Sweet dreams and guillotines

Blank Page

Chapter II
Dead Flowers

A Pumpkin On My Mailbox

A pumpkin on my mailbox
So everyone will see
That no matter what the season
It's always Fall to me

98

I Had A Cat

I had a cat
But then she died
We keep her in
Formaldehyde

She goes with us
Near and far
But stays inside
Her big glass jar

The Little Frightened Ghost

The little frightened ghost
Didn't like the nights
He wasn't like the rest
And never caused a fright

He frightened very easy
He startled rather quick
He didn't like surprises
Nor a joke or trick

He stayed up in the attic
With his lantern light
Reading antique books
And staying out of site

The little frightened ghost
Wasn't like the rest
He wasn't into haunting
And causing such unrest

The Haunted Ballroom

There's a ghost dancing in the ballroom
There's a ghost hanging from the drapes
There's a ghost swinging from the chandelier
Eating purple grapes

There's a ghost off in the corner
Eating someone's brain
Washing down the frontal lobe
With a glass of pink champagne

There's a ghost in fancy shoes
There's a ghost in borrowed socks
There's a ghost out in the hall
Picking all the locks

There's a ghost reciting poetry
While floating through a wall
There's a ghost with an old time telephone
Trying to place a call

There's a ghost in formal clothing
There's a ghost in fancy dress
There's a host who's a ghost and a ghost of a host
And a ghost who's a ghost hostess

There's a butler with a serving dish
And I can see right through his head
He claims to be a ghost himself
But he's only partially dead

There's a ghost with a knife and a fork
There's a ghost with a fork and a knife
There's a ghost arguing with her husband
And a ghost fighting with his wife

Gruesome Lester

There was a man
Named Gruesome Lester
Who had a sore
That he let fester
He had a sore
That he let ooze
To which his wife
Was not amused
He had a sore
That he let swell
Much to the point
It begun to smell
He had a sore
That he let blue
Until it popped
And ran with goo
There is a man
Named Gruesome Lester
Who has a scar
He doesn't pester

Allister Picked A Scab

Allister picked a scab
He picked a scab indeed
It left a hole so dark and deep
That nothing could be seen

Until a bug crawled out
Another one or two
One by one they crawled right out
He didn't know what to do

They covered up his body
Crawled up his face and head
They picked and bit him nice and clean
'Til he was finally dead

Creepy Moon

Creepy moon
Don't stare at me
I was sleeping peacefully
I can see you
Through the trees
Looking down
Right back at me
Now, I'm awake
And I can't sleep
Creepy moon
Don't stare at me

Adrift On My Sea

Dark and alone
Here on my own
Sometimes it feels
Like I don't have a home

All by myself
One book on a shelf
Sometimes it seems
Like nobody will help

But what have I done
To go ask someone
To give me some time
And a piece of their sun

So I don't have to be
Adrift on my sea
Without any help
Alone with just me

Drown

Up and down
Round and round
My emotions
Won't slow down

Back and forth
Left to right
There is just
No end in site

Close the door
Put out the light
Try to tell
My brain goodnight

Count to ten
Or ninety nine
But that won't slow
My frantic mind

Up and down
Round and round
My emotions
Won't slow down

Another Time

The sun may fall
The moon may rise
But we don't have
To say good-bye
So long my friend
Will do just fine
Until we meet
Another time

Fragmented People

I am just a fragment
Made complete by
The fragmented people
Around me

Black Is My Favorite Color

Black is my favorite color
My favorite color indeed
Don't give me Blue, yellow or green
For that's not what I need

Black is my favorite color
I guess it's just my mood
If you were me and I were you
You would wear it too

Macabre Mary

Macabre Mary
Was scared of the light
And she made quite sure
To keep out of site

She hid in her dress
Her scarf and her hat
All of which were
The darkest of black

She wandered the halls
The chambers the nook
Avoiding the help
The butler, the cook

She roamed the gardens
The streets and the parks
But only when they
Were sufficiently dark

She had a black cat
Dark glasses on tight
A parasol shade
To simulate night

She stays in a room
Most of her days
Avoiding the sun
And it's menacing rays

Her candles quite dim
Her curtains pulled tight
Anxiously waiting
For day to be night

The Morning After

The morning after
A very sad day
My Jack-O-Lantern
Is rotting away

Last night it was orange
Round and full of life
A freshly carved face
And a candle for light

Now it is black
White, green and dark blue
The morning after
Was not kind to you

Dead Flowers

Ms. Beatrice wandered
Her gardening beds
She picked all the flowers
That were dying or dead

She picked all the flowers
Decrepit and cold
She knew they were lifeless
And could never grow old

She put them in vases
All over her room
Although they had passed
And would never bloom

She still saw their beauty
Though departed and dead
That beauty lived on
And never did shed

Ghosts And Goblins

Ghosts and goblins
Goblins and ghosts
I don't know
Which I fear most

One you can't see
Though they do not hide
The other you can't
Unsee if you try

Crypts And Coffins

Crypts and coffins
And Coffins and crypts
I saw a ghost
And my heart went skip

Skips and coffins
And Coffins and skips
Scared me to pieces
Now I'm dead in a crypt

Casting Spells

Mason Bell
Is casting spells
Something he can't do
That well

Breaking mirrors
Crossing cats
Turning people
Into rats

Turning puppies
Into poo
Watch out now
He's after you

Box Of Curses

Box of spirits
A box of curses
Evil spells
And witchy versus

Splintered bones
Bat near death
A jagged tooth
And black cat's breath

Any spell
Kind or cruel
I cast you now
To close my school

Bring the zombies
Raise the dead
So I don't have to
Leave my bed

Boogers And Blood

If you stick your
Finger in too deep
Boogers and blood
Are what you'll reap

Myrmecophobia

Myrmecophobia
And the feeling it grants
Is the fear that I get
Being eaten by ants

Ear-Pierced Holes

Can somebody
Just answer please
Why ear-pierced holes
Smell like cheese?

Spooky, Creepy, Eerie Clown

Spooky, creepy, eerie clown
I don't wanna see you around
Above all when the sun is down
Spooky, creepy, eerie clown

Something's In My Room Again

Something's in my
Room again
In the corner
Where it stands
When I turn
The light switch on
That something in
My room is gone

Plaster's Falling

Plaster's falling
From the ceiling
Something's upstairs
Stomping creeping

But if I should
Go up and see
The thing upstairs
Will then see me

Best to leave it
Stomp alone
And I'll just sit here
In my home

Plaster falling
From the ceiling
I'm downstairs
So it won't see me

Zombie Ficus Tree

There's a zombie ficus
In the corner of the room
Right behind the couch
In its potted little tomb

One day we heard something
Dragging across the floor
The ficus dropped its branches
And crawled right out the door

It stopped to turn around
That is when we ran
But it only went back in
To get the water can

Toilet Poem

There was a boy
Named Martin Doo
Who flushed the toilet
With his shoe

Then ran and stood
Ten feet away
He was scared
He'd fall and stay

In the toilet
Down the drain
In the sewer
To remain

Dog Poem

Dog on the carpet
Dog on the floor
Dog lying down
Blocking the door

Dog on the couch
Dog on the bed
Dog laying down
Its butt by my head

Dog in the kitchen
Dog in the den
"Mom, the dog is
Throwing up again!"

Dog in the bathroom
Drinking from the bowl
Dog's trying to lick me
"Why's his slobber cold?"

Little Squirrel

Little squirrel
Playing in the road
I go left
And left he goes

Little squirrel
Playing in the street
I go right
And so does he

Little squirrel
Get out of my way
The street is no place
For you to play

Spider On The Ceiling

Spider on the ceiling
Spinning his way down
Down into my cereal
Where he'll finally drown

Spider in my cereal
Floating all around
Try to eat around it but
Impossible I found

Spider in the milk
Lost inside the white
Didn't see you on my spoon
I just took a bite

Batty Maddie

Maddie was a little bit batty
We didn't care or mind
So when we found she slept upside down
We figured that it would be fine

My Eight Legged Friend

My eight legged friend
In the corner of my room
She inside her living space
I inside mine too

My eight legged friend
Nestled in her web
Looking down upon me
As I'm in my bed

My eight legged friend
Was the only friend I had
Until she got discovered
And squashed dead by my dad

Here Lay Mr. Grant

Here lay
Mr. Grant
He went out for a picnic
And was devoured by ants

Cockroach Feet

The pitter patter
Of cockroach feet
On the floorboards
Under me
I try to fall
But I can't sleep
When all I hear
Are cockroach feet

<u>Dead Moth Remains</u>

Dead moth remains
In a lamp above my bed
I'm awake but they're asleep
Mostly because they're dead

Dead moth remains
In a lamp above my bed
I really should just clean them out
But they might spill on my head

<u>Undone</u>

There once was a boy with a fear
A fear that wouldn't subside
He was always afraid his knot would unbraid
And his navel would come untied

Good Witch, Bad Witch

Good witch, bad witch
I don't know which one is which
And I don't know just what I did
For them to turn me to a pig

It Must Be Halloween

Monsters in the mausoleum
Horrors in the halls
Ghosts outside the rusty gates
It's beginning to look like Fall

Zombies in the neighborhood
Hear the children scream
Witches take to flying high
It must be Halloween

Witches' Brew

Witches' Brew
Hallows moon
Halloween
Is coming soon

Vampire bites
Bats take flight
On a spooky
Hallows night

Witches' Life

Witchy morning
Witchy day
Living life
My witchy way

Witch's broom
Witch's hat
Life is pretty
Good like that

Condemned Carly

Poor condemned Carly
Was burned at the stake
For being a witch
Inside the wrong state

She told her accusers
She said to them all
She'd be back as a ghost
And haunt them next Fall

Esther Witch

Esther Witch is watching children
Esther Witch is making stew
Esther Witch is very hungry
And she's looking right at you

Coffee

Hazel the witch
And her wicked posse
Won't lift a broom
Till they finish their coffee

Ms. Macabre Maddie

Ms. Macabre Maddie
Buried her dolls
Inside the backyard
With their clothes and all

She said a few words
Cried in her shawl
Then went to the store
And bought a new doll

Like A Ghost

Chrissy stumbled
Chrissy fell
Chrissy drowned
Inside a well

She got right out
Kind of, almost
She floated out
Just like a ghost

Skeleton Tree

Skeleton tree
You've lost your leaves
They're scattered on the ground

Fall has come
And you're undone
You're just like me, I've found

Skeleton tree
You've lost your leaves
Your birds have flown away

You're just like me
Alone to be
For no one wants to stay

Three Little Skeletons

Three little skeletons
On their very own
Not quite so happy
In their very own bones

They took themselves apart
And they moved some things around
Made a trade or two
And used what they had found

A bone right over here
A bone right over there
They thought they were complete
Till they found there was a spare

They came apart again
Yes, they moved some things around
And they found that they were happy
Just the way that they were found

The Grim Mortician

The grim mortician
Felt sad inside
Everyone he touched
Had already died

And left him alone
In his sad little room
Without anyone
For him to talk to

Coffin Canoe

Martin had a coffin canoe
He took it to every port he knew
He was the captain, but he had not a crew
Sailing across the ocean blue

Chapter III
Ashes To Ashes

13 Ghosts

Thirteen ghosts in a dark parade
Thirteen ghosts sing a serenade
Thirteen ghosts in a haunted show
The pirate ghosts says "Yo, ho ho"
Thirteen ghosts on a hollows eve
Thirteen ghosts, count 'em ten plus three
Thirteen ghosts flying in the sky
One falls back from a fear of heights
Twelve ghosts creeping, on down the street
One stays back to rest its feet
Eleven ghosts hiding in the trees
One falls out because it sneezed
Ten ghosts in a church bell tower
Bells too loud for one ghost prowler
Nine ghosts carving up pumpkin heads
One got bored and went to bed
Eight ghosts haunting a house of four
One by accident went next door
Seven ghosts at the grocery store
One got stopped by the sliding door
Six ghosts took a ride on bikes
One crashed hard into a trike

Five ghosts hiding in the pale moon light
One saw its shadow and then took flight
Four ghosts count them one and three
One blew away in a heavy breeze
Three ghosts playing tag in the street
Car came and knocked one off its feet
Two little ghosts, in a dark parade
The sun came up, and it fled for shade
One little ghost, left all alone
Sad and lonely it went home

Some Ghosts

Some ghosts are just mean and scary
Some are still just deeply buried
Some ghosts like to hide about
And come out when the moon is out
Some ghosts want to cause a riot
But this ghost likes to sit here quiet

Grandpa Vampire

Grandpa vampire
Left his tomb
And wandered out
Into the gloom

He found a house
He snuck inside
He found a victim
Sleepy eyed

He went to strike
He went to bite
But suddenly
He caught a fright

He left his teeth
Forgot his dentures
Didn't take them
On his venture

Still at home
In his tomb
Where he left them
In his room

Now he can't strike
And he can't bite
Looks like he won't
Eat tonight

Grandpa's Ear

Once upon a time
There was a little jay
That flew into my grandpa's ear
Intending just to stay

She made herself a nest
From strands of tangled hair
The hair was from my grandpa's ear
But willingly he shared

She laid a dozen eggs
They grew and flew away
She left her nest and cleaned the mess
But grandpa's hair remained

Peter Jebb

Peter Jebb
Sneezed a web
Of tangled mucus
From his head

Strands of yellow
Strands of green
A mucus laden
Horror scene

Peter Jebb
Sneezed a web
Of tangled mucus
From his head

Popcorn Dish

Sister drooled in the popcorn dish
They used to crunch, but now they swish
Sister drooled in the popcorn bowl
I wish she had some self-control

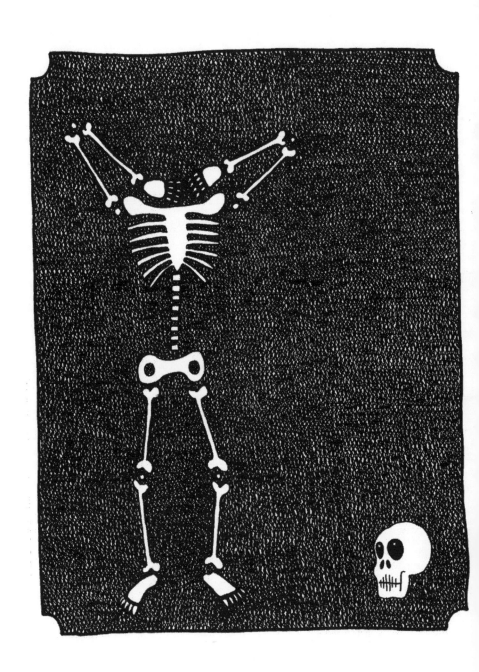

Lost My Head Again

I guess I lost my head again
I don't know where, I don't know when
I hope that it's not gone for good
I better check the neighborhood

If you see my head out and about
Give me a holler, give me a shout
Won't make a difference though, you see
My body can't hear, my head can't flee

Perry, Perry Pumpkin Head

Perry, Perry
Pumpkin head
Couldn't fall
Asleep in bed
His head was round
And way too odd
For him to sleep
Just like a log
He always had
His candle on
Most things do not
Burn that strong
Deep inside
He had a flame
Unfortunately
Not a brain

Putting Things Together

Putting things together
Things that are apart
Things that went unnoticed
Sometimes from the start

Things that may have weathered
Somewhere on the way
Putting things together
Hoping they will stay

Close To The Bottom

Close to the bottom
Here in the dirt
Some would believe
It's what I deserve

Believe if you want
Believe if you will
But we all have our holes
We dig and we fill

We All Have Scars

We all have scars
No matter who you are
No matter where you're from
And no matter how far

We all have scars
Locked behind the bars
Of our own made prison
Just wishing on some stars

We all have scars
No matter where they are
No matter how you got them
They will always be ours

We all have scars
No matter who you are
No matter how you hide them
We always have scars

Alison Sodden

Alison Sodden
Was nowhere around
People were always
Letting her down
Empty promises
Unfulfilled hopes
Never a yes
But always a nope
She ran to the woods
And hid in the trees
Where she could hide
Herself in the leaves
She cried and she cried
Her tears fell like rain
They showered, they fell
Again and again
She tried hard to stop
She thought that she must
Her eyes wouldn't open
And started to rust

They just wouldn't open
So she pried and pried
Out of frustration
She cried and she cried
Alison Sodden
Was nowhere around
Engulfed in her tears
She finally drowned

Rainy Day Poem

It's just another rainy day
I guess I won't go out to play
I'll just read a book and stay
In my bed not far away

From the fire and its heat
Warming up my hands and feet
What a cozy winter treat
While it's raining in the street

Warming Bones

Sitting by the fire place
Trying to warm my bones
There's a chill outside this space
I'm so happy to be home

Watching Clouds

Watching clouds
Passing by
Looking up
I wave good-bye

I don't go
Anywhere
And those clouds
Do not care

They float on
Peacefully
And they know
Where I'll be

Bugs

Underneath the midnight sky
I chose to take my sleep outside
But something's crawling up my side
Over my face and on my eyes
I think they're trying to get inside
They scratch and bite and try and try
Through my nose they seem to find
A way to finally get inside
Now they're in and I can't hide
And to this day they still reside
In my head behind my eyes
So if you chose to sleep outside
Cover your nose, your ears and eyes

Blood Or Ketchup

Blood or just ketchup
I cannot recall?
And why is it on
My shirt after all?

Where did it come from?
This isn't fun
Blood or just ketchup
My mind is undone

Bobby Grew Tired

Bobby got tired of hearing
So he cut off both his ears
But then he grew tired of seeing
So now he can't see or hear

Edmond Had A Hammer

Edmond had a hammer
He also had some boards
And he had the right amount
Of nails to cause discourse

His parents were unhappy
And worried most quite often
They didn't know why he was
Only building coffins

Antique Vase

Victor broke an antique vase
And all were quite concerned
It seems it wasn't a vase at all
But someone's antique urn

Mortuary Bob

Mortuary Bob
Had the coolest car around
Everyone would stop and stare
When he drove through town

The old folks all seemed scared
They all ran to hide
But Bob just drove his hearse through town
Asking "Hey, who died?"

Reckless Witch

Reckless witch went flying high
Hit an airplane passing by
Now she's stuck and can't let go
Grasping to the airplane's nose

Captain Dread

Captain Dread
Lost his head
Upon the seven seas

They threw
His body overboard
His head was not retrieved

It rolled
About the cabin
With every single wave

His head
Is still upon the ship
And rolling to this day

Index Finger

Marco had an index finger
Biggest one I've ever seen
He pointed it at everyone
With whom he disagreed

Matilda Jones

Matilda Jones
Makes tea from bones
Grounded up and steeped

She takes a
Platter and a cup
Where people tend to sleep

Cemeteries
Make here merry
While she sips her tea

Matilda Jones
Makes tea from bones
Of her enemies

Billy Rudd

Billy Rudd
Was big and mean
And he hated
Everything
He always acted
Big and strong
But there was just
One thing wrong
Deep inside
His angry self
Was a heart that
Needed help
A heart that needed
A little love
Even if from
Billy Rudd

The Lonely Coatrack

The lonely coatrack
Stood by the door
Year after year
And a decade before
It stood and it waited
It stood or it sat
With never a coat
A scarf nor a hat
It stood in the winter
And there in the fall
Walked passed by many
Walked passed by all
Ignored by the family
Ignored by the guests
Ignored by the help
If you haven't yet guessed
Never a jacket
A mitten nor glove
This poor lonely coatrack
Was just never loved

Even a pick staff
A cane or a pole
Would fill in the void
That tormented its soul
No umbrella for rain
In the wintering gray
Nor a parasol waiting
For a hot sunny day
Just a lonely ol' rack
Out by the door
Year after year
Like the decade before

Bathroom Floor

Struck in the head by the bathroom door
Now I'm sprawled out on the bathroom floor
Wish they'd clean this place frequently
I wouldn't be laying in somebody's pee

Skid Mark, Toilet Bowl

Skid mark
Toilet bowl
Brown swirl
Down the hole

Slide marks
Brown stain
Porcelain
Toilet drain

Was here
Before me
I only
Went pee

If you're
Waiting for
Me at
The door

Don't you
Blame me
After
I leave

Skid mark
Toilet bowl
Brown swirl
Down the hole

I Have A Secret Power

I have a secret power
A magic sort of deal
I always pick the shopping cart
With the jammed up wheel

Everyone's aware
They just stand and smile
When they hear me squeaking down
Every single isle

Sidewalk Earthworms

Sidewalk earthworms
Burnt beyond a crisp
Baked under the summer sun
Into a blackened twist

Sidewalk earthworms
Crunch beneath my feet
They sound like they would be something
That I would like to eat

Go Away

I don't know how to tell you
I don't know what to say
Please don't go away mad
But please just go away

<u>Squeaky Hinges</u>

Squeaky hinges
Never lie
Never keep
The truth inside
Never silent
Standing by
Squeaky hinges
Never lie

<u>I love you….</u>

I love you as wide as my arms can go
I love you more than you'll ever know
My love for you just grows and grows
I love you as wide as my arms can go

Two Little Ghosts

One little ghost
Found another little ghost
Now those two little ghosts
Have become quite close

Love For Us All

Cold, dead and buried
She wasn't yet married
So she found herself a groom

In a neighboring grave
She dug the remains
Of a poor old gentleman's tomb

Lifted and carried
And newly reburied
After the exhausting haul

Now she lives in a tomb
With her very own groom
Isn't' there love for us all?

212

Ghost Cookies

Grandma is a ghost these days
And often visiting
But when she bakes us ghost cookies
We just don't taste a thing

It's ok and we don't mind
They won't go to waste
Since Grandpa is a ghost as well
And he just stuffs his face

Ghost In The Window

There's a ghost in the window
That no one else can see
He waits for everyone to turn around
And shows himself to me

When I go to tell my friends
To turn around and see
The ghost inside the window disappears
And no one else believes

Mirror Ghost

There once was a ghost
Who avoided all mirrors
And though he was clear and couldn't show flaws
He still remembers the pain they would cause

Musical Chair Ghosts

The ghosts in my house
Love to play
Musical chairs
Every day

They wait for supper
We go to sit
They pull the chairs
And the floor we hit

The Tidy Witch

The tidy witch
Was very clean
All her dishes
Were pristine

All her clothes
Were folded neat
And on her bed
A brand new sheet

And of course
Her floor was swept
Thanks to the magic
Broom she kept

Wrinkled Cape

The vampire with
The wrinkled cape
Could never keep
It smooth or straight

Couldn't keep it
Hanging flush
No matter how he
Pulled and brushed

He tried and tried
And failed and failed
To keep it sleek
To no avail

No one took him
Serious
But they found him
Curious

While he stood there
By the bed
As his victims
Scratched their head

Watching as he
Fought his gown
Smoothing
All the wrinkles down

Stomping, stepping
Patting down
But those wrinkles
Stay around

Till he's finally
Had enough
Storming off
In such a huff

The vampire with the
Wrinkled cape
Left again
Before he ate

Catacombs

When I die and turn into bones
Put my remains in a cavernous home
A cavernous home for my raggedy bones
A cavernous home, yes indeed I will go
Under the streets in the dark catacombs
Under the streets for my raggedy bones
Don't take me to Cairo, don't take me to Rome
Take me to Paris and the dark catacombs

Ashes To Ashes

Ashes to ashes
Dust to dust
Leave if you have to
Go if you must

Blank Page

Chapter IV
Let's Get Married On Halloween

Let's Get Married On Halloween

Let's get married on Halloween
With the silver stars and the
Skeleton trees
(Where) the people don't throw rice
Only jelly beans
So let's get married on Halloween

234

Sleeping In The Graveyard

Sleeping in the graveyard
Sleeping with the dead
Sleeping with the skeletons
Cozy in their beds

I never had a bad dream
I never had a fright
I never had a thing
But a restful night

Ghost In A Jar

Sofia had a game
That she loved to play
She made it up all by herself
One cold and rainy day

She collected empty jars
That people threw away
And took them to the cemetery
Where she found a grave

The jar went in the ground
She put it upside down
And pushed it down into the dirt
And inch below the ground

She knocked upon the grave
Woke the spirits up
And when they rose up from the dirt
She scooped the jar right up

She screwed the lid on tight
And much to her delight
She had a ghost inside the jar
To take back home that night

She put it on her shelf
With all the other ones
Thirteen angry ghosts in jars
Doesn't sound like fun

As if you didn't know
Or couldn't quite recall
You cannot keep a ghost inside
Anything at all

Sofia didn't care
She didn't have a clue
Stealing spirits from their graves
Is something you can't do

They slipped out of their jars
While she was in her bed
Every single ghost she took
Flew into her head

Late into the night
She woke up with a scream
For every single ghost she took
Had haunted all her dreams

<u>Mason Licked His Finger</u>

Mason licked his finger
To see what he last picked
His ear or nose or something else
But what on earth was it?
It wasn't sweet at all
It wasn't even tart
It tasted rather salty
I guess that is a start

Odds And Ends

Odds and ends
Bits and pieces
Little things
Found in creases

Under pillows
Under beds
Stacked in closets
Up to my head

I've a problem
I'll admit
I keep everything
That I get

Hair In My Ears

Hair in my ears
Hair in my nose
Hair on my cheeks
And the tips of my toes

But there is no hair
Where I wish it would grow
On the top of my head
Why is that so?

Let's try again
Let's get it right
I know we can
I'll walk right through
That door again
Let's start all over
If we can

Happily Never After

There is no happily ever after
There never was
We were lied to
By the people who love us

80 Years

You have about 80 years here
Sounds like a lot but it's not
You have about 80 years here
Make the best of what you've got

Happy Me

I'm not trying to be different
Nor difficult, you see
All I'm really trying to do
Is be a happy me

The Crow And The Rainbow

The crow and the rainbow
On opposite sides
Wings of a feather
Against beams of light

The crow to the rainbow
Let out a cry
"Why won't you share
With me your light?"

The rainbow to the crow
Said with a sigh
"It's up to you crow
To find yours inside."

Cemetery Statue

Cemetery statue
In the same old place
Staring at the same old graves
With the same old grace

Cemetery statue
Is it safe to say
If you were not made of stone
You would walk away?

Sixteen Little Pumpkins

One little pumpkin
Alone in a patch
Two little pumpkins
Now we've got a match
Three little pumpkins
Growing on a vine
Four little pumpkins
In the sunshine
Five little pumpkins
Winter's coming soon
Six little pumpkins
In the autumn moon
Seven little pumpkins
Ready to be plucked
Eight little pumpkins
Children run amok
Nine little pumpkins
One looks all alone
Ten little pumpkins
This one's coming home

Eleven little pumpkins
Ten and just one more
Twelve little pumpkins
Hollowed to the core
Thirteen little pumpkins
On a hallows night
Fourteen little pumpkins
With a candlelight
Fifteen little pumpkins
It has been a dream
Sixteen little pumpkins
Happy Halloween

Three Little Zombies

Three little zombies
One, two, three
Each one looking for
Something to eat
Something to feast on
Something to chew
Hope that it isn't
Me or you
Something to grab and
Hold very tight
Something to snatch
And something to bite

Three little zombies
One, two, three
Each one looking for
Something to eat
Something to gnaw on
Something to dine
Hope that is isn't
Me or mine
Something to snack on
And swallow
I think that it's time
For me to go

Zombie, Zombie

Zombie, zombie,
I've gotta say
I've got a brain
That's wasting away
I don't use it much
So I'll sell it today
Just name your price
The amount that you'd pay
I can charge you now
Or just lay it away
It will be all yours
As the receipt will now state
There are no returns
Nor a trade or exchange
So sink in your teeth
Before it's too late
Or you can save it a bit
And let it ripen with age
It's yours to decide
I cannot think straight
For I haven't a brain
Since it's there on your plate

Bones

My bones are achy
My bones they all creak
My bones are frail
From my head to my feet

My bones are a cage
Surrounded by meat
They keep me from being
Just a blob on the street

I moan and I shriek
When I stand from this seat
I wake from a nap
And I can't move a thing

I'm done with these things
These old bones I mean
I'm tossing them out
In the morning, first thing

Next time you see me
Next time we meet
You'll have to say hi
To the blob in the street

Broken Days

Broken hearts
Broken dreams
Broken fingers
Broken seams
Broken words
Broken ways
Keep on making
Broken days

This Is For Someone

This is for someone
I do not know who
It may be for me
It may be for you
But you're doing fine
And we're doing good
The best that we can
The best that we could
Nobody's perfect
Not me and not you
This is for someone
I do not know who

What Do You Do?

What do you do
When you feel so blue
And you're walking around
In the same old shoes?

You don't belong
And it seems so long
That you can't remember
When things weren't wrong

It's lonely here
And it's hard to steer
Passed the crushing storms
To the distant clear

What do you do
When you feel so blue
And you're walking around
In the same old shoes?

You push along
And rewrite your song
Then the right folks will
Come and hum along

Who You Are?

When things look bleak
And things look dark
Do not lose site
Of who you are,
Who you've been
And want to be
The highest thought
Of what you see
In your mind
And in your heart
That determines
Who you are
Not the weather,
Not the tide
But all the light
You have inside

I Love You So Much

I love you so much I want to kiss you
I love you so much I want to hug you too
I love you so much I want to eat you
Put you in my mouth and turn you into poo

Bubbles In The Bath

Bobby's making bubbles
While he's in the bath
He isn't using soap
You can do the math

Leland Dug Himself A Hole

Leland dug himself a hole
And lived there with the bugs
Worms and things and in-betweens
Living in the mud

He had nice conversations
He had some games to play
But most of all he didn't have
Grownups in the way

Garbage Can Lollypop

Garbage can lollypop
I noticed you weren't done
I saw you in the trash
Glistening in the sun

Someone quit you way to soon
And threw you in the heap
Would you mind if I inclined
To take you all for me?

I promise that I'll treat you right
And finish every lick
And when I'm done I'll toss away
Just an empty stick

Last Christmas I Got….

Last Christmas I got
A great ball of snot
Under the Christmas tree
I later discovered
It came from my brother
It was from he to me
It was big, it was round
It was great, it was brown
And about the size of a roast
Oh how it smelled
When picked up and held
Right at the tip of one's nose
My brother, he laughed
When it finally unwrapped
And sat all alone in its box
I'd much rather have
In a brown paper bag
A case of the measles or pox

But that's not the case
On this very day
I'm stuck with a box full of snot
But this I don't mind
For next Christmas time
I shall finally strike right back
For under the tree
To my brother from me
Shall be a great pile of.........
Something.........I'm not really sure yet

Bubble Gum Shoe

I'm so stuck on you
My bubble gum shoe
Since the day I put you on
And we walked into that goo

It's like we both knew
It would be just me and you
From that day on
My bubble gum shoe

Rub A Dub Dub

Rub a dub dub there's a hair in my tub
And it's sailing around by my feet
It's curly and brown and it will not sink down
I'm trying so hard not to scream
There are not many things in life or in dreams
That can scare a man from his skin
But a curly remain of a hair by the drain
Rattles my bones deep within
I splash and I paddle but I'm losing this battle
For now it's right up to my knees
What I need is a bucket, I don't want to touch it
Can somebody rescue me please?
Now, isn't that somethin' it's up to my button
And working its way to my chest
It's a nightmare of sorts, it stays right on course
And it's driving me into a wreck
I scream, "What the heck, it's up to my neck!"
But I hear not a peep of reply
I say with regret, "Oh that's just what I get
For not scrubbing the tub since July."

Now here it is May, and I'm caught in this fray
And I fear that it's fight to the death
I need to calm down, stop splashing around,
Think and take a deep breath
But as I inhale, like wind to a sail
The hair plays more of a kite than a boat
And casts down on me like waves from the sea
And now it's stuck in my throat.

Buzz Away Fly

Buzz away, buzz away, buzz away fly
Your twenty-eight days are over, just die
I hear you, I see you, I swat low and high
Buzz away, buzz away, buzz away fly

Tip Toe Mosquito

Tip toe mosquito
Where did you just go?
I did see you from
The side of my eye
Tip toe mosquito
I hope you do know
I see you again
You're going to die

Mosquitos In The Lantern Light

Bug bites and parasites
Mosquitos in the lantern light
You've never been my friends before
And you're not my friends again tonight

Up, down, side to side
And swapping to the left and right
Hitting everything in site
Except mosquitos in the lantern light

What bad things have I done in life?
Past, present or current times
To be a victim of such strife
To mosquitos in the lantern light.

You Wrecked Me

You wrecked me
You tore me apart
You ran me over
And backed up the car

Orange Peel Gentleman

Orange peel gentleman
Wrapped around himself
Who wants to spend the time
Peeling off his thick skin
Just to hopefully be
A wedge inside his circle

Little Pink Clouds

Little pink clouds
Floating away
Maybe I'll see you
Some other day

Little pink clouds
Gone to give way
To dark rainy clouds
Heavy and gray

Hello Up There Midnight Moon

Hello up there midnight moon
I thought that I would be alone
Out here in the streets tonight
Running further from my home

Hello up there midnight moon
Can you stay and listen please?
Do not wonder off to far
Let me see you through the trees

<u>As Far As My Arms Can Go</u>

I love you as far as my arms can go
I love you as tight as my grasp can hold
I love you more than you'll ever know
I love you so much that I let you go

Rubber Bat

Once there was a rubber bat
Bouncing from a string
Thumbtacked to the very top
Of somebody's ceiling

The bat was very sad
And longing to be free
And not just packed inside a box
And hung on Halloween

Milford The Cozy Ghost

Milford is a cozy ghost
He's the one I like the most
In life he was a man well fed
In death he's like a cozy bed

Fluffy, round and soft as air
Doesn't fray and doesn't tear
Milford is a cozy ghost
He's the one I like the most

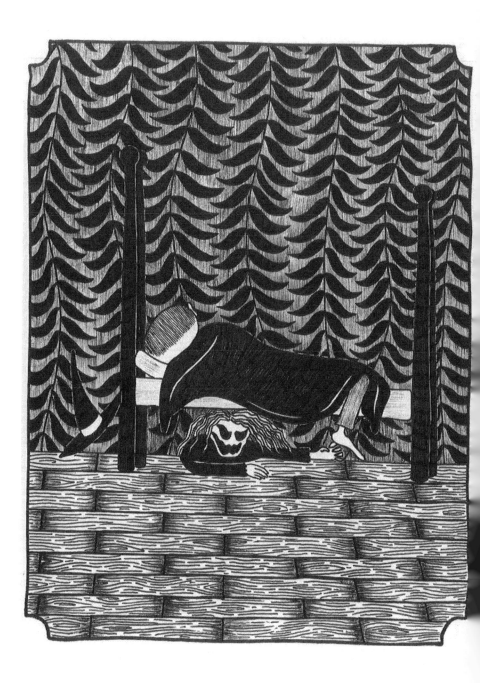

Dangling Little Feet

Late at night
When all is dim
And all small children
Are tucked in
In their beds
And off to sleep
With those dangling
Little feet
Hanging from
The mattress side
Waiting for
A big surprise
The wickedest
Of wicked creeps
The witch who steals
Children's feet

Levitating Molly

Levitating Molly
Tried to go to sleep
But every time she laid in bed
She floated several feet

She knew there was a ghost
She knew her house was haunted
But one night of restful sleep
Was all she really wanted

The Old Tangled Tree

Carla carved her initials
Into an old tangled tree
The tree got very angry
And grabbed her by the feet
Its branches were thick and sharp
As it pulled her from the ground
And there was poor old Carla
Hanging upside down
It whispered in her ear
Its tone was cold and deep
"I like to eat small children
Who carve their names in me."

Victoria Drabs

Victoria Drabs
Eats her scabs
Contrary to her mom and dad

Eats them whole
And not in halves
Says they're really not that bad

Breakfast, dinner
Lunch and snack
Sits alone and chews like mad

Wipes the crumbs
Off with a rag
Little Miss Victoria Drabs

Windowsill Cobweb

Windowsill cobweb
Moving in the breeze
Caught between the glass
And the window screen
Mom can't clean it
So she lets it be
Windowsill cobweb
Moving in the breeze

Mummy With A Runny Nose

Mummy with a runny nose
Couldn't wipe it on his clothes
Didn't have a handkerchief
Couldn't lift it with a sniff

One solution he did have
Wipe it on a handy rag
Didn't think it through although
Now he's soaking head to toe

Batsicle, Ratsicle

Batsicle, ratsicle
Catsicle stick
I'm freezing pets
For a hot summer lick

Don't care if they're hairy
Or come in a shell
Don't care if they're rotten
Decrepit or smell

Batsicle, ratsicle
Catsicle lick
I'm freezing pets
On a popsicle stick

Ghost Bat

Ghost bat flies in the middle of the night
No one can see him but it's quite alright
He's just a ghost so he doesn't bite
Ghost bat flies in the middle of the night

Ghost In A Box

There's a ghost in a box
And a box in a room
The ghost in the box
Comes out with the moon
Yes, the ghost in the box
Comes out with the moon

Now the ghost in the box
With the moon in the sky
Comes into my room
But just to say "Hi"
Yes, the ghost in my room
Comes in to say "Hi"

And me in my room
With the ghost by my bed
Was startled at first
Now calm in the head
Yes, rattled at first
By the ghost at my bed

So the ghost in a box
But now in my room
Who came to say "Hi"
By light of the moon
Is still at my bed
Under light of the moon

So now me in my bed
Still scratching my head
Pondering over
That which was said
Yes, thinking it over
The "Hi" that was said

So the ghost in a box
In the moon glowing light
Has pulled up my sheet
And kissed me goodnight
Yes, tucked me in gently
And kissed me good night

So now me in my bed
Still scratching my head
Pondering over
The kiss that was shed
Pondering over
What happened in bed

There's a ghost in a box
And a box in a room
The ghost in the box
Comes out with the moon
To tuck me in gently
So sleep can resume
To kiss me good night
By light on the moon

Plan My Funeral

I'm going to plan my funeral
While I'm still alive
And tell my friends and family
That they should all stop by

We will all get together
Have coffee or wine
Sitting, Laughing and talking
Reliving past times

The End

Made in the USA
Middletown, DE
11 November 2022

14621866R00184